Whoooo Knows
and Other Backyard Tales

Patrick Holliday

For Susan,

Wishing you well now
and for the future!
Hope you enjoy the stories; :)
some are from the backyard.

Sincerely,

Pat Holliday

Snow Eagle—Mechanicsville, PA
ISBN: 978-0-578-82676-9
Library of Congress Control Number: 2020925459
Title: *Whoooo Knows and Other Backyard Tales*
Author: Patrick Holliday
Digital distribution | 2020
Paperback | 2020

This is a work of fiction. The characters, names, incidents, places, and dialogue are products of the author's imagination, and are not to be construed as real.

Dedication

To Rob & Jen, for their ideas in creating the artful illustrations for this book that bring the stories to life!

Prologue

We should look at nature and observe how the species interact with each other, we'll see the birds, the beasts, the fish, and all of the furry creatures of the planet still following what was preordained from the beginning of time.

The animals still live as they were created, continuing to survive, reproduce and living within their specific species. We should take the time to observe and marvel at their interactions to one another, and in part to their humorous actions in their day-to-day life.

The following stories are both fact and fiction, and I leave it up to you as the reader to determine what you believe. But most of all, I hope you will enjoy and appreciate nature's creatures of the land.

Center Ring

Here, where shadows and trees reflect each other so perfectly, who is to say what is land, what is sky, or what perfection it is that springs a gray squirrel's body from oak tree to pine, many feet in the air?

The squirrel does not think of himself as one of the many possible acrobats plucked from the circus of life, or to live out his days as a performer in nature's arena. To him, it is no surprise when he crosses the shadowed lawn, to see mesmerized cats stare as he climbs up the vertical trunk of the world.

He is like one of those ancient creatures found on hidden cave walls, tiger mouthed, vulture claws, with bulging eyes. How calmly he goes about business of foraging for food or performing one of his circus acts for all to see.

No human passage concerns him, compared to the safety of the trees, his size absorbed by the trees, barely noticed as we pass beneath. Ever on the move, he keeps a watchful eye for hawks and owls, lest he be their afternoon delight.

So, the wind-roughened fur of the squirrel brushes against the sharp edge of the tree bark, as he moves from limb to limb in his quest for nuts, or perhaps to practice his circus act. Perfectly camouflaged above or below, he sails from tree to tree like a trapeze artist thrilling all who would notice his daring.

And we, who inherit the earth for all its magnificent beauty, do not feel the green clouds of the treetops, or the green blankets of grass as do the squirrels. How they convey nature's spirit of life and vitality, not accepting their short life span, but living each moment to its fullest as nature intended, in center ring.

The Injured Crow

As a young boy many years ago, I found a black crow that had injured its wing and could not fly. It was on a warm summer's day that I brought him home in hopes of helping him, as I could not bear even at that age of seeing one of nature's species suffer. It made no protest as I picked him up as his wing hung helplessly down from his body, I carefully held him in my hands as I gently walked home making sure that the wing was not bumped by any object.

I found a big metal tub that I lined with some towels and placed him in on his stomach so as not to re-injure the wing. Examining the wing I could tell that he had been shot breaking the main bone of the wing, which rendered the wing useless. I made some splints from parts of my model airplane collection, and carefully splinted and taped the bone together. Most of this knowledge came from my friend, a veterinarian who gave me instructions over the phone on the correct procedure.

I left a cup of water next to him in the tub and fed him some through an eye dropper. The next morning, he accepted some food, some blue berries and bird seed. He seemed in good health at that moment, other than the wing, his eyes were bright and clear. I tried to talk to him, he looked straight at me showing no fear or aggression, and I sensed that he was unsure of his surroundings.

I later borrowed a cage so that I could put him close to a window, so that he could look out and see the world. He loved the light, he would swing his head from one direction to another, and again, gazing slowly and deeply. There were other times that I would put him outside so that he could watch other birds, of course the cage protected him from nosey creatures that wanted to know him too well.

Many weeks went by as we got to know each other, he would actually show recognition when I came up to the cage by hopping up and down. He would eat food out of my hand and then take a drink of water, and then would cackle and do a little dance for my benefit.

One day I noticed that he was flapping his wings in unison, I think telling me that he was ready to fly again. I took him to my veterinarian friend for a checkup and was told that the wing had completely healed and was time to let him go.

He was of course, a piece of the sky, his eyes said so. This is not necessarily fact, but a part of knowing that it was his time to be free again. So, on a bright late summer's morning I took out into a big field, opened the cage, and lifted him out with my hands. He looked at me with those shiny black eyes so eager to fly again, as to say to me, thanks for saving me for one more flight. With that I lifted him up into the air, and then released him to the sky he loved so much. I felt sadness in letting him go as he had become one of my many numerous pets, but a great sense of joy in knowing that I had helped one of mother nature's creatures.

The Little Goslings

One bright sunny morning as I was driving on a quiet country road, I spotted a gaggle (group) of Canadian geese clustered around a pond in the middle of a grassy field. Suddenly in front of me walking, or should I say marching alongside of the road were several families of geese. Apparently, they were taking their little ones for a short stroll before heading back to the pond, for a quick dip to cool themselves off after the long walk.

I pulled my car off to the side of the road so that I could watch this very entertaining spectacle, as the various families led their little ones along the road.

It was heartwarming to see the mothers keeping their children in line, one after the other, like little toy soldiers marching along. There were four families of geese; the first had the mother and four goslings, (baby chicks,) the second family had six goslings, the third had five goslings, and the fourth had seven goslings.

Watching them proceed slowly down the road, I could imagine them with a drummer leading the way as the little chicks marched in step. Suddenly, the last gosling of the first family decided to break ranks and cross the road. The mother would have none of this, as she chased after the little guy and grabbed him by the tail and brought him back to the other three goslings. As you can imagine, there was much squeaking going on with the other chicks wondering if they should test their mothers, or just stay in line.

The mothers patiently led their little ones down the road and over the field to the awaiting pond, which of course caused much excitement among all the little goslings. They talked among each other about the fears of going into the water, wondering if they would float or sink. One of the mothers spoke up and said, do not worry children, you will not sink, your soft little feathers will keep afloat. All you will have to do is watch us grownups, and do what we do, and you will have lots of fun paddling around the water.

The last thing I saw as I started to drive away, was 22 little goslings having the time of their lives swimming around and chasing each other, while all the time letting out quacks of joy.

The Bull Frog

The bull frog was just sitting on a large green lily pad sounding off with its baritone voice, emitting jug-o-rum, jug-o-rum continuously throughout the day and night. I do not know if he were calling for a future mate, or if he were just singing to anyone who would listen that he was lonely and wanting company.

This bull frog, who I will call Otis, was a big fellow, weighing around 2lbs. with a shiny green coat with brown spots, and large round ears. This was not your normal bull frog, no sir, he looked like he was on stage waiting to perform. He pranced around the lily pad, all the time bellowing out his jug-o-rum call, stopping now and then waiting for applause.

The more I watched Otis, the more I liked him, He was king of his very own domain, and he had more to offer than just survival, he had showmanship. If I really concentrated, I could see him with a top hat and cane, white bow tie and sneakers, dancing his way through the pond. Through the day I watched Otis perform and sing as he sat on the lily pad, often I would applaud his acts, and at times he would acknowledge my approval with a jovial bellow.

Time flew by as I sat there watching Otis all the time mesmerized by what he did, when we were interrupted by an aggressive female frog, a frog I will call Sally, was in the eyes of frogs, an attractive frog. Well, she just captivated Otis to such a degree that he became discombobulated, meaning that his mind became mush. He started to tremble and stammer, could no longer bellow out his jug-a-rum calls, instead, he fell madly in love with Sally. As I got ready to leave, I watched Otis and Sally nose to nose having an understanding as to the future for both of them.

I will tell you all that the ending turned out very well, Otis and Sally got married in the pond with many guests in attendance. They went on to an incredibly happy life together and had many tadpoles who to this day swim in the pond.

My Friend Petey

When I was a little boy, I lived on a small gentlemen's farm where we raised a small sampling of various animals. There was a horse, some chickens, a couple of ducks, a Billy goat, a few sheep, and an occasional stray cat.

I would always look forward to the springtime, as that would be the time for the birth of new baby lambs. To see them run and jump around the fields was a spectacle like no other. They would at times play follow the leader, each jumping over an imaginary obstacle to see who could jump the highest, and at other times racing to see who was the fastest.

During the birthing time for sheep, I was asleep in my bed when I was awakened by a noise coming from the barn. It sounded like a bass drum with intermittent beats, not something you expect to hear coming from the barn late at night. I quickly put on some clothes on the run and ran down to the barn to investigate the noise, and much to my dismay I saw fleecy, a mother sheep head butting a newborn baby sheep up against the barn stall wall. I immediately gathered the little lamb up in a blanket that was nearby and proceeded to take the little one up to the house and into our basement. There I put him into a dog basket which I lined with more blankets and stayed with him the rest of the night to make sure he survived until morning. I do not know the reason that the mother was trying to kill the lamb, perhaps she sensed that the creature was weak or sick, or that she could not take care of both lambs.

The next day I called my friend the veterinarian to see what could be done to save the little lamb, in hopes that I could nurse him back to health. He suggested that I get a baby bottle and start feeding him with warm milk, which I tried to do several times a day. It was late spring, and although I was still in school, I would feed him in the early morning and after school in the afternoon. My mom would take over during the day, along with my dog Windy, who would keep him company.

Petey, a name I gave him started to thrive on the milk and attention, and though wobbly at times, began to walk around the basement. The vet suggested that I take him outside in the sun, so that he would not contract rickets. He responded to the sunshine and fresh air and became much more confident in his movements. As the days and weeks passed Petey became stronger and energetic and was itching to join the other lambs during their daily romp. When I thought he was strong enough, I would let him join the others during their play period.

Although he still wanted to be bottle fed, he had started to supplement the milk with some grass. As he grew, he would follow me wherever I went in the fields, constantly wanting me to pet his head and his nose. He grew rapidly over the next couple of years and was my constant companion anytime I was in the fields. One time when a neighbor's dog tried to attack me, Petey rushed at him butting him head on, just to protect me. The dog was so surprised that he turned tail and ran off in a hurry, and I never saw him again.

Every day that I would walk through the field to feed the other animals, Petey would follow me wherever I went, sometimes even pushing me with his nose. Sometimes he would play hide and seek with me, hiding behind a building and then running up and playfully butting me from behind. This game would on for many months, until it finally became too rough of a game. He also became aggressive to anyone else who would dare enter the field, that I had to consult with the vet to see what I should do. He explained that Petey had grown up and was no longer a little lamb, that he had become a ram that now needed to be with female sheep to calm his aggressions. He recommended that I find a farm that raised sheep, that would take him in as part of their family.

Well, the time came after I had found a sheep farm several miles away, that agreed to take Petey as an addition to their flock, and I would have to say goodbye to my friend. One bright sunny day after I had made arrangements, the farmer came with his truck and loaded Petey into the back for the long trip to his new home. As I said goodbye to him with tears in my eyes, I petted him and said I will come and visit you when I can. Petey looked at me with those shiny black eyes as if to say, thanks for all you did for me and I will miss you.

The few times that I was able to visit Petey at his new home, he always spotted me and would come running over to the fence and wait for me to rub his head. He seemed to enjoy his new home, especially all of his new girlfriends. I felt privileged to have been his friend, and happy that he grew from a sickly lamb to a healthy strong ram, and he will always be one of my fond memories.

Foxy the Fox

Foxy was a beautiful fox, with auburn coat of hair and a long bushy tail. Her face was long with a black shiny nose, long white whiskers on both sides of her mouth. When she ran across fields, her short legs moved quickly, so fast that they appeared as blurs to the human eye. She was referred to as foxy because of her cleaver way of getting what she wanted, like food in the name of chickens, ducks, geese, and rabbits.

Foxy spent much of her time hunting at night, but on occasion would go out in the daylight if she were still hungry. She lived in what is known as a fox hole in the middle of the woods, she had it well furnished with straw, grass clippings, and pine needles. Fox was hoping that someday she would have a family of little pups, and of course, a Mr. fox to help around the den.

One late afternoon Foxy woke up and stretched her short legs and thought, I must find a better way to get food other than what I have been doing lately. So, one evening she decided to visit the local farmer who raised chickens and cows and planted corn and wheat to feed his animals. She approached the farmer in her best seductive manor and said, sir, if you will allow me to guard your hen house from evil predators like bad foxes, fisher cats, raccoons, and other villains; all that I ask is one chicken a day as payment. The farmer agreed to that arrangement, and so Foxy guarded the hen house every night thereafter, and happily took her payment of the chicken home to feast on in her den.

We all know of course that nothing stays the same forever, and Fox was no different, she met a very handsome Mr. Fox, shiny auburn coat, long bushy tail, white whiskers twice the length of hers. Well, it was not long after that they became husband and wife, destined to spend the rest of their lives together sharing whatever nature had to offer. It was not much later that little fox pups arrived in the den, six to be exact, three little girls and three little boys. Now the problem was that Fox's one chicken per day would not be enough to feed them and the six pups, so they had to come up with a better plan for more food.

So, the next day they both went to the farmer and explained their problem, and the farmer was incredibly pleased to hear that Foxy had both a husband and six little pups. He stood there awhile scratching his head and thinking, and then he said, Fox, instead of just watching my hen house, why don't you and your family move into my farm and keep me company. In return, you and your family will be able to have all the food you want without wondering where the next meal will come from.

So, Fox and her family moved into the farmer's land, and with tummies full, lived happily ever after.

The Beach Beggars

Sitting by the cliffs in southern California, overlooking the Pacific Ocean, I noticed a lot of activity of little creatures as they scurried among the rocks. These creatures are better known as California ground squirrels, a mixture of gray, light brown, and dusky hairs, with a bushy, sometimes flat tail.

These little critters are shameless beggars, constantly looking for handouts from anyone who would offer. They scurry from burrow to burrow, always on the lookout for their predators; eagles and rattlesnakes to name a few. I have watched them dive into trash cans, wondering how they climbed out after searching for a few little snacks.

On one particular sunny day as I sat by the cliffs, I noticed some rather robust activity going on at the cliff's edge. It seems a group of squirrels had gotten together for their version of a football game, which of course drew the attention of both humans and other creatures. They would line up with several squirrels on each side of an imaginary line and using a peanut the received from a human as the ball, proceed to play the game. This was no ordinary football game, no way, it was comical to watch as one group would try to run the ball; I mean peanut, to the other end of the small playing field. They would kick and bite one another as the squirrel with the peanut tried to run through the other team's line, all the while making clucking noises as they tried to stop the runner.

The game seemed to go on for quite some time, but I noticed that most of the squirrels were beginning to tire and became bored. Some scampered off to their burrows for an afternoon nap, others climbed up the cliffs to beg for snacks from the people parked along the road viewing the ocean. With their hot tail swishing, they were trying to tell the people, look at us, we are cute, throw us some food.

So as the sun started to fade into the Pacific Ocean, the little beggars having stuffed themselves with all the free snacks, scampered off to their family burrows for a night of rest. Tomorrow was another day for them to beg for food and entertain the people with their little shows.

The Fisher Cat

Every morning the cat with his shiny black coat steps stealthily along the grassy lawn, as though he found the day brand new and wonderful, and without a doubt, especially made for him. The birds stare, and the mice run for their lives as he marches along his chosen path on his soft padded paws. His goals and intentions are not of the birds or mice, but the collection of little goldfish in the neighbor's reflecting pool.

"Oh yes," his black shiny head seems to say, this will be yummy, here is breakfast and lunch both, and dinner as well. When he sees me daring to look at him, he lift's his tail as to say to me, butt out, this is my private safari and I do not need company.

It was only a few moments past the sun's rising, which meant that he had the whole morning to fish and dine to his heart's content. To watch him stick his paw gingerly in the water attempting to catch one of the goldfish was fascinating, as he would pull back and shake his paw as though the water was on fire. He would stand there balancing on three legs while trying to snare a little fish with his right front paw, and sort of jump each time he touched the water.

This ritual went on for some time, until finally he caught one with his claws, quickly flipping it up into the air. Putting his little foot on it to hold it still, he looked over at me as to say, see I am a great hunter, so there!

34

The Trial

O n a sunny morning in early summer, I was driving along a scenic country road observing the beauty of the land. As I continued to drive slowly through the countryside, I took in the sights of many of nature's creatures conducting their day's activities. Cows were grazing lazily in the meadows, horses were frolicking in the field, as birds and geese passed by overhead.

Continuing to drive slowly along a deserted country lane, I suddenly caught an activity out of the corner of my eye that made me pull the car over to the side of the road and stop. There in a sparsely covered field were a group of black crows congregating in a large circle, and as I exited the car the noise emitting from the circle was almost deafening. Upon closer observation, I noticed a single crow in the inner circle surrounded by hundreds of noisy fellow crows, all addressing their cackles directly at him.

Not understanding crow speak, I intently watched the proceedings as they continued for close to a half hour. From what I could tell from the body language of the crows in the circle, it appeared that they were conducting a trial directed at the crow in the middle. Apparently, the accused had done some despicable act against the flock, and it was now his time to atone for his actions. It was obvious that the circle of crows was the prosecution representing the entire flock, while the single crow in the middle was the defendant without any defense counsel.

After almost thirty minutes of noisy cackling by the circle of crows, and as the crow in the middle stood silently without as much as a peep, the circle of crows in unison silently turned their backs to the defendant. With that, the defendant, obviously found guilty, flew off by himself, banished from the flock.

It was apparent that nature like humans, also has laws protecting itself from those who would conduct themselves in an unacceptable behavior in their society.

The Great Hunter

At the edge of the woods, a small honey colored fox was slinking along, as he cautiously put one short leg after another on last year's spent leaves. You could tell that he was on a mission, food was his goal, as he had a mate and pups back in the den to feed, and failure was not an option.

There were few creatures stirring except for some deer grazing on the lawn, and birds chirping as they gathered material for their spring nests. But this fox had only one thought on his mind, a hunger for squirrels that would not be satisfied until he caught one.

He stood motionless and listened and looked in all directions, including the many trees around him for a sign of squirrel activity. You could tell that this fox was no ordinary hunter, he displayed a keen since of awareness of his surroundings as he stealthily proceeded with the hunt.

It became clear as I watched him in his hunt, that the squirrels would not be an easy prey.

Every time he would get ready to pounce on one, they would scamper up a tree chattering all the while. One squirrel appeared to be teasing him by climbing down a tree within a few feet of him, and when the fox moved, the squirrel would quickly climb back up, turn around twitching his tail as he chattered noisily, as to say, ha-ha, you did not get me!

It was apparent that this was not to be the day to catch a squirrel, but as he headed home unsuccessful in his hunt, much to his surprise, a mole popped up in the middle of the lawn. In a flash he sprung forward and pounced on the mole, successfully clutching it in his teeth. Happy that he finally caught a meal for his family, although small, it would hold them until tomorrow's hunt.

Foxes are one of nature's amazing animals, cunning and persistent hunters, and this one was no different. Although he is small in size, in his mind I am sure he thinks he is a wolf that all should fear.

The Backyard Deer

I saw their hoofprints in the leaves and pine needles behind the house and knew they had ended their long night sleep under the pine trees. Walking slowly like they were going for an early morning stroll, they headed towards me as though I was no threat to their existence.

They came slowly across the lawn and looked at me standing under the trees, and shyly they stepped closer and stared from under their thick eye lashes as they nibbled some damp blades of grass.

This is not an imaginary story, but it could be. It is about reality and Mother Nature's interaction with us humans. Finally, one of them, I know for sure, would have come to my arms. But the others stomped their hoofs on the grass as a reality check, and off they went for their daily stroll through the trees.

Just when I was ready to dismiss their visit and go about my day, a little one appeared at the edge of the woods. My eyes caught his about the same time, the reaction was a sign of recognition of past acquaintance. Low and behold, this was the youngster I rescued from his entanglement in a wire fence a few days ago.

He looked at me with his coal black eyes, his dark lashes flicking like wiper blades as his eyes went from me to his mother retreating into the trees on the other side of the lawn. He was a beautiful little creature with a white diamond marking on his nose, a white chest plate, and a white tipped tail that reminded me of a bunny.

Tail whipping back and forth, up, and down, he raised his nose to sense who this familiar human could be. Satisfied that he knew who I was and that I was no threat, he bounded off towards a reunion with his mother. As he ran past me, he gave me what appeared to be a smile as he kicked up his back legs as to say, you are ok as a human, and thanks for the other day.

Life is always a challenge for both humans and animals from the day they are born until the day life ends, but in between those two spans is an obligation for all of us to share life and kindness with all of Mother Nature's creatures, including the deer.

The Squawky Scrub Jay

A friend of mine on the west coast was enjoying her rose garden one morning, when she spotted something in the driveway. She discovered that it was unfortunately a dead baby bird, a tiny hairless newborn. As she was afraid that her dogs might find it, she picked it up, wrapped it in a paper towel and carried it away.

Later that day while in her house, she heard very loud squawking outside. She went to investigate and saw a beautiful blue scrub jay sitting on the balcony railing outside of her living room, emitting several very loud squawk, squawk, squaw, and man was it loud. She stared at the scrub jay from inside of her house, as if to ask why? A truly angry bird to be sure.

My friend then moved to a different room, the kitchen this time. The jay flew over to the railing outside of the kitchen window and continued to look and squawk at her. She questioned as to why? What had she done? Then it hit her, had the jay been watching and had seen her pick up her baby and take it away? Was that the reason for the tongue lashing? It made sense.

This behavior continued incredibly for 5 days, at every window, and sometimes even during the night. If she went to the kitchen, there she would be, cursing at her. No matter what room she went to, the scrub jay would find her and continue her verbal abuse.

My friend felt so bad about the scrub jay's baby that she thought maybe she could appease her by setting out a substitute baby for her to morn over, so she took a furry little cat toy and placed it on a table outside near the railing. That did not make her feel any better, as she tilted her head and seemed to say, are you kidding me? She knew that she had no doubt insulted the mother bird.

My friend decides to consult a bird expert, so she googled Scrub Jay behavior and came up with Cornel University Ornithology Department, "a study of bird behavior." She emailed them about her dilemma, never expecting a reply to such a ridiculous situation.

The next day a wonderful explanation was mailed back to her. The ornithologist explained that the bird's behavior had nothing to do with the baby bird or her. In fact, this scrub jay was likely a male, not a female. She learned that the squawking behavior is common during the mating season. The scrub jay was not seeing her at all, but was seeing his own reflection in the window, thinking it was another scrub jay competing with him for the territory, hence the tirade.

Shortly thereafter all became silent, apparently the scrub jay must have finally conquered his rival.

The Hawk and I

One glorious day I decided to rent a glider at the local airfield to enjoy one of my passions, this is a hobby of soaring using a sail plane, commonly known as a glider. This is a small plane with a long wingspan, without an engine, usually seating one or two people. The glider is towed aloft to around 4000 feet and then the tow rope is released, and the glider soars on its own relying on the air currents to keep it aloft. It is a lot like sailing a boat on the water, as the boat also relies on the wind to keep it moving, both require knowing how to navigate the wind and air.

Enough of the explanations on the art of soaring, let me begin by saying that being up there in the clear blue sky and white puffy clouds, is the most peaceful experience you will ever have. If you are lucky, you can stay up in the air one to two, maybe three hours if the air currents are there. You might ask how high you can go, and that again depends on the currents, on a warm summer day with the heat radiating off the ground causing the air to rise, you can go up to ten thousand feet and beyond.

So, on this magnificent sunny day, I arrived at the airport around noon time to take advantage of the warm air and low winds. I did the required walk around ground preflight of the glider, and then hooked the tow rope from the tow plane to the glider. After climbing into the cockpit, I strapped myself into the seat with the seat belt and closed the canopy. I then waved to the tow plane that I was ready to launch, and so we proceeded to taxi to the end of the runway. A few minutes later we started down the runway with the glider bouncing along behind the tow plane, like a puppy chasing after a ball. Once we got up enough speed, we became airborne, with the glider and me following at a short distance behind climbing counterclockwise until we could reach 4000 feet altitude.

Once we reached the 4000-foot altitude, I reached down and released the tow rope by pulling on the release arm. With a wave from the tow plane by moving his wings side by side, the glider started to climb like an elevator going to the next floor. I settled down for what I thought would be a quiet time soaring through the calm blue sky, as I listened to music on my cell phone playing John Denver's song.

I am an eagle. All of a sudden as I glanced out of the canopy, there on my left was a magnificent hawk, his dark brown feathers sleeked close to his body, his wings spread out as he soared close to my left wing. As we soared together through the sky, he would turn his head toward me, as if to say, high their friend, good day for flying isn't it?

So, as I would gain altitude with the help from the air currents, so would my friend the hawk, no matter if I went up or down, he would stay with me. I decided to see how long he would follow me before he became tired of the game, so I would turn left and he turned left, I turned right, and he turned right. This exchange went on for at least a half hour or more, or least in seemed like it. As I started to lose altitude, I needed to head back to the airport. I looked out of the glider to find my friend the hawk still there next to my left wing, so I smiled as I waved to him to let him know that it was time for me to go back to my nest, ending another day of beautiful flying. He gave me one last look as to say, nice flying with you, and then he turned away from me and flew off into the clouds.

This true story of friendship between a human and a bird pf prey, gives meaning to the close kinship between man and nature, that we have more in common than most people think.

Rocky the Raccoon

One warm spring day as a young boy, I came across a quick running, white frothed stream, among the moss-covered islands of wet rocks, a small bundle of fur. I knew from pages of a book that it was a baby raccoon; he was crying a pitiful sound of fear and loneliness. The strong sound of his little voice was not easy to describe, I had to lean in to try and understand what the little guy was trying to say. What was in his frame of mind, or at least interpret by the tone of his cries.

I picked up this little bundle of wet fur and placed him in my baseball cap, as I headed home to give him a warm place to dry out and hopefully become less frighten to his surroundings. I found a small carton that I lined with towels, and at the same time placed a small stuffed animal in it to give him company.

The challenge was teaching him to eat, as raccoons are nocturnal carnivores that feed mostly on fruits, nuts, and small animals. So, I provided him with some grapes, nuts, and a little raw hamburger, and settled down to watch him eat. To my surprise he would not touch the food, it was after some research that I found out that raccoons need to wash their food first. So, I put a small bowl of water next to the food, and as you can guess, he went to town first washing the grapes and then the nuts.

It was a soul stirring event watching him pick up the grape in his tiny paws, and then dip the grape in the water, and then shake the water off before he began to eat. I named him Rocky since I had found him among the rocks, and because the first few weeks he would rock back and forth trying to get stability in his legs.

Rocky grew fast, he had a ravenous appetite, I was constantly looking for grapes and nuts. As hard as I tried, I could not get him to be friendly, although I felt from the look in his eyes that he appreciated my kindness.

So, the day came when it was time to take him back to his native habitat, a place where I knew other raccoons lived and hunted. I felt a deep sadness as I released him into the woods, although I also felt a sense of pride that I had saved him so that he too could become a grownup raccoon.

He turned to me once to look at me as to say, thanks friend for all you did, and then he scampered off into the woods hopefully to join others of his kind.

There are times that I still see him, and whenever I open a book and see a picture of a raccoon, I see him, a little grey ball of fur with black frightened eyes, now burning with love.

The Kitty and the Lady

The lady worked at a manufacturing facility surrounded by other factories and warehouses near some railroad tracks and overlooked the nearby Pacific Ocean.

She would often spot stray cats in the parking lot, and sometimes around the other buildings. Sometimes she would see a medium size, very skittish black cat.

She would pass by the floor-to-ceiling window of the lady's office, so many times she had an excellent view of her. She was a beautiful cat, sleek and black hair with bright green eyes.

She decided to start leaving out bowls of food and water for her, hoping to be able to watch her more closely. For several months she fed the cat and watched that nothing would harm her. When the lady went on vacation, one of her co-workers would take over food and water duty so that she would never go without food and water to drink.

"Black Kitty" came every day. She would stop at the window, look in and see the lady at her desk, and as the lady would slowly approach the window, she would run off. Through time Kitty would gradually allow the lady to come closer to the window, until finally she could stand inside and watch her feed. Occasionally, Kitty would look up from the bowl, and as though she could read the lady's mind, she could tell that this human meant no harm to her.

Some mornings the lady would go outside to fill the bowls and noticed Kitty lurking in the nearby bushes, watching her and waiting for her breakfast. Kitty finally allowed her to get within a few feet, and although progress had been made

The lady resigned herself to the realization that she was a wild cat that would never be tamed.

The one day "Black Kitty" passed by the window with 4 tiny black kittens in a row following behind her, and so "Black Kitty" became "Mama Kitty," but then, that is another story.

The Kitty and the Lady
Part 2

So, one day the "Animal Lady" so called by her co-workers because of her intense love for animals, was busy working at her desk when a frantic co-worker came to her upset that he thought he heard a kitten crying underneath a truck in the parking lot. The lady dashed to the storage room and picked up a box, grabbed a towel from the kitchen that she put in the box and hurried outside to the parking lot.

Sure enough, the man was able to reach under the truck and carefully hand her the tiniest kitten she had ever seen, solid black with tiny green eyes. She could not walk, and apparently had injuries that could not be determined at the moment. The Lady immediately called the closest vet in the area, and with a short time was waiting for the veterinarian's verdict. The vet confirmed that she had been injured, and evidently left behind by her mother as part of a new litter. The vet suspected that the kitten had a broken pelvis or broken hip, perhaps as a fall.

They wanted to keep her overnight for observation, so the lady left her with the vet in her little box.

The vet did x-rays and confirmed that she had a broken pelvis. No one knew how long she had been under the truck, but she was in bad shape, undernourished and suffering severe dehydration. So, after work the next day the lady picked her up from the vet, who exclaimed that she did not expect the kitten to survive the night and that she should not bother to name her. But she added "although kittens can be amazingly resilient, sometimes this type of injury can heal on its own."

The lady took the kitten home that night, placing her little box in a quiet place in the spare bedroom. She was so worried about her and wanted her to survive, that she decided to defy the veterinarian and named the little kitten "Hope." Twice through the night she went in to check on her, placing her hand on her tiny body to make sure she was still breathing, and she was!

The next day the lady took Hope to work with her to make sure she continued to drink water, and some mother's milk that she bought at a pet store. She attempted to feed her using an eyedropper but found the Hope's mouth was too small to take the end of the eyedropper. So, she went back to the pet store and bought a tiny little syringe, that was small enough to do the job.

Though out those first few days at work, the lady fed her hourly, and Hope gradually started to take the milk, and she seemed to be on the mend. So, she set up a little litter box in her office so that Hope would not have to go outside, and at the same time making sure she was getting her most important feeding of milk. Occasionally she would go over to the window and watch Mama Kitty feed; was there a spark of recognition?

Everyone at work just adored Hope and would come and visit her several times a day. The lady initially did not intend to keep her, because at the time she had 2 big dogs at home who thought cats existed solely to be chased by them. She kept telling herself that there was no way could it ever work out, having Hopey (her nickname) and the 2 dogs.

But it did not take long before Hopey and the lady had bonded in a special way. She would spend the days with her while at work, and at times ride on the lady's shoulder and fall asleep while she walked around the office. Hope continued to grow and thrive, and had the tiniest little meow ever heard along with being so sweet and innocent.

Then came the day when the lady decided to formally introduce Hopey to her dogs, as she knew it had to happen sooner or later if all were going to live together. Oh yes, by that time she had decided that she could never give her up.

She temporarily fenced off a hallway from her spare bedroom in her house with a five-foot wrought iron fence. Hopey and the dogs could see each other, but no one felt threatened. Well, within 10 minutes Hopey had hopped the fence with the greatest of ease, like a flying Wallenda! No problem!

Obviously, she was a little kitty miracle who survived a horrible ordeal but was one of those resilient ones the vet talked about. She was her rescued kitty whom she called her little gift from God and changed the lady's life in ways she could not have imagined. Hopey stayed tiny and skinny, sleek, and black, with beautiful green eyes, sweet and adorable, and to this day continues to love her as no other.

The girl and the Deer

One warm sunny afternoon, a young girl was taking one of her frequent jogs around a residential area where she lived. At the same time without her knowing, a young female deer was making her regular tour around the development enjoying all the juicy delights found on the various lawns. The deer absolutely loved nibbling on the rose bushes, the beautiful flower gardens, and other tasty shrubs.

Later in the day as the deer continued to sample the treats in the neighborhood, she saw the young girl running down the street. Thinking that the girl might want some company as she ran alone, the deer decided to catch up with her and keep her company, which seemed like a good idea at the time.

As the deer started to trot after the girl, she noticed that the girl was looking back at her, and then suddenly stopped to stare at her. The deer saw that the girl had a frightened look on her face, which totally confused the deer who only wanted to be friendly, after all, it is usually the deer that is frightened. As they stared at each other, which seemed like forever, the started to run again. The deer thinking this may be fun, and a break from all the nibbling, started to trot after her, not knowing the girl was terrified of her. The girl continued to run faster and faster, all the time screaming as though the deer was going to attack her, which really confused the deer who only wanted to play.

Continuing to scream and yell at the top of her lungs, the girl ran to the closest house and pounded on the front door. When a lady answered the door to see what was wrong, the girl in hysterics asked if she could call her parents to come and get her. After calling her parents between sobbing telling them what happened, she hung up the phone. The lady asked her what was so terrifying to cause her to react this way, and if she wanted her to call the police. The girl explained all the events that just occurred leading up to her knocking on the lady's door, and that she was afraid that the deer meant to harm her.

Little did the girl know that the deer only wanted to play, and had no intentions of harming her, and by running away only hurt the deer's feelings. But there is a happy ending to this story, the deer went back to enjoying the treats offered in the neighborhood. The girl finally calmed down from her experience with the deer, and soon went off to college with her stuffed teddy bear and lived happily ever after.

Alfred the Squirrel

This is a unique story about a chance encounter between me and of Nature's little creatures, resulting in a short but beautiful relationship that truly touched the heart.

It all started when I saw several squirrels playing on the lawn and got the idea that maybe they would appreciate a treat. So, I went back into the house and gathered some mixed nuts that I had on the shelf and proceeded to throw them out onto the lawn for the squirrels to eat.

As I headed back to my front door with an almost empty bag of nuts, I noticed one particular squirrel following me from a safe distance. When I reached the door, I turned around and knelt down, and with my hand extended I offered some nuts to him. He sat there twitching his tail, staring at me with those tiny coal black eyes, apparently afraid to get close to me although at the same time intently looking at the nuts I was holding in my hand. Sensing that he was not going to get any closer to me, I tossed the nuts in front of him and closed the door as I entered the house.

The very next day a tap at the front door got my attention, and when I did not immediately get up from my desk, there again was a soft tapping at the door. I got up from my chair and peered out the front door window, not seeing anyone I went back to my desk. Again, the soft tapping emanated from the door, a persistent tap as though someone or something was growing impatient. I opened the door and looked out, and as I looked down, much to my surprise I saw a tiny grey squirrel looking up at me with two coal black shiny eyes.

His tail was twitching as he sat on his haunches, his front paws were held out in front of him as though he was begging for food. Having spoiled so many squirrels in the past with food, I could only guess he had been a reciprocate of some of those treats. I found some soy nuts that I had fed the squirrels during an earlier time and proceeded to drop them at his feet. Instead of reaching out to eat them, he instead looked up to me with incredibly sad eyes as if to question my actions.

Not knowing what was wrong with my actions, I knelt with some nuts in my hand and offered them to him. Believe it or not he cautiously started to nibble from my hand, occasionally, tail twitching, he would look up at me as if to express his gratitude for the treat. Having finished two handfuls of nuts, he looked up at me, swished his busy tail and scampered off chattering all the way.

The very next day my furry little friend returned, it was late afternoon and I had just returned from a short trip when I heard a faint tapping at the front door. Having stocked up on walnuts and other goodies, I was quite prepared to treat my new friend.

As I opened the door, Alfred, a name I decided to call him was sitting on the red brick walkway eagerly awaiting my treats. He looked up at me with those shiny black eyes, his little ears wiggled in consort with the swishing of his bushy long tail. His small body expanded and contracted in his anticipation, as he waited for me to extend my hand with the treats. After eating a handful of nuts, he looked up at me with his cute little pointed face and proceeded to chatter away.

I knelt again with some walnuts in my hand to see if that was what he wanted, or if he was just trying to thank me. He proceeded to stuff the walnuts in his cheeks, and when he could stuff no more, he touched my hand with his cold little nose as if to thank me, and then bounded off across the lawn.

As Alfred and I became closer friends, I noticed certain peculiarities that seemed to surface whenever he showed up for his treats. He sometimes displayed a belligerent attitude along with moments of anger, that would become apparent during his incessant chattering at me.

The visits continued to progress, and each time I would be confronted with more and more verbal abuse each time I opened the door. It was like he was telling me he did not appreciate the days I was not there to feed him, or I was holding him up from other things when I did not readily open the door.

On one visit I knelt and extended my hand with nuts to satisfy his lordship's appetite, all the while looking into those deep black shiny eyes. He rapidly devoured the nuts, his bushy long tail swishing in all directions until all the nuts were gone. As he finished the last nut, he backed up a few inches and started to chatter a mile a minute, first on all four feet and then to sitting upright balancing on his tail. I assumed from all the noise from his mouth he was agitated that I had no more nuts and was telling me he wanted more. I tried to tell him I was out of food and that he would have to wait until tomorrow, and perhaps in the meantime he should take an anger course for squirrels. He replied with a series Kuk, Kuk, Kuk sounds, and scampered off into the woods.

Near the end of his visits to me he showed up one day looking like he had been in a fight, both ears were nicked and bleeding, a chunk of hair was missing from his tail, and he had a slight limp. I have an idea that his anger got him in trouble with the other squirrels, and that I was probably the only friend he had left. From that day on he was never quite the same, he shows up sometimes without a sound from his little mouth, nor a sparkle in his eyes. There was a sadness that emanated from his tiny body, as though he knew our time together was short lived.

A couple of days later I found his small body in the middle of the lawn, he had apparently died sometime during the night, alone and cold. I wrapped him in a small towel and buried him in the ground with a bed of pine needles, along with a few of his favorite nuts.

There is nothing more rewarding than sharing kindness with one of Nature's creatures, I received as much enjoyment as I hope I gave to my friend Alfred, I will miss him.

The Caged Lioness

One warm summer day I was visiting a local zoo to enjoy the large variety of animals represented from all over the world, with special interest in the large cat family. There were Tigers, Cheetahs, Lions and Pumas, with the Tigers being the largest weighing up to 660 pounds. The Lion typically weighs between 330 to 550 pounds, with the male reaching the high end of that range.

The lions were lounging around the shallow pool within their closure, some cooling off in the water while others were napping. The Cheetahs were resting up in the tree, taking a midday nap after enjoying a delightful lunch. The Pumas, or mountain lion as known in the US, was hiding behind a large bolder, as they are not known for being a sociable animal.

As I continued to watch with interest the various cat families and their lazy activities, I became aware of a female lion in cage off to the side of their enclosure. She was pacing back and forth in front of the metal bars that separated her from the world, all the time looking out at the people who stop to stare at this beautiful animal. Under her golden tawny brown skin flowed a hidden power as she placed one paw after another moving back and forth, all the time as she looked at me with those big black eyes.

I sat there while I sipped an iced tea, wondering what the lioness was thinking as she paced back and forth. Were those shiny black eyes reflecting the streams and jungle of her native Africa, or was she missing not having the opportunity to have little ones to teach how to hunt. In her native land she was always able to roam and explore the sub-Saharan African plains, it was her country and she dreams to be there again. If you look closely into her eyes, you will see the sadness she feels of being caged and not free. She only wants what we humans want, to be free to live and explore life without the constraints of cages and bars.

Pigging Out

He was not your ordinary pig as pigs go; he came into this world with a voracious appetite for many things in life, much to the disdain of his siblings.

Max was his name; he was born several years ago in the early spring, one of eleven piglets. Seven of which were girl piglets. From the very beginning Max would push his brothers and sisters out of the way during feeding time, he always wanted more than his fair share. It got so bad that his mother scolded him one day, she said if you do not change your ways, you will wind up being called a hog.

As the years went by Max grew up and became an active member of the pig society, continuing his opulent lust for the better things in life. As nature intended, Max met a beautiful girl pig of outstanding attributes that he began to pursue. The relationship between them grew and in time became one of loving intensity, and they began to share many intimate times together.

Of course, Max being the over indulger that he was, always wanted more, whether it was time together, more wine or more love, he always wanted more. One day his friend, her name was Matilda, said, Max, don't you think you have had enough love for now? You are starting to behave like a hog instead of a pig.

Well Max suddenly recalled what his mother had said to him several years ago about never getting enough, that at that tender age he was behaving like a hog. So, Max not wanting to lose his sweet Matilda, he made a promise to himself that he would no longer behave like a hog, instead he would act like a normal pig with a hog's appetite.

So as the descriptions of his actions may have changed, Max and Matilda continued to enjoy a loving and fulfilling relationship together, Matilda controlling the overindulgence with an occasional snip which put everything in perspective.

The Squirrels of Autumn

Among the fast-growing bed of leaves on a crisp sunny fall day, a multitude of frisky squirrels play out their last rites of summer. Some are just gathering nuts for storage for the long winter ahead, as others take time to play in the trees and on the ground.

How interesting and amusing it is to watch them in their various antics, some performing as acrobats and others as athletes competing for who knows what.

The constant chatter of the squirrels is accompanied by the overhead squawking of the geese as they fly by, accented by the sun filtering through the quickly turning leaves casting their multi-colored glow on the performer's stage below.

Suddenly, out from the colony of squirrels came two furry gray creatures, hell bent on rough housing with each other. Chattering and swishing their tails, they spared with each other as though they were tiny boxers in a ring. Standing on their hind legs, balanced by their bushy tails, they slapped at each other with their tiny front legs.

If one was counting, the squirrels probably went several rounds of sparing with each other before calling it a draw. Suddenly during the face off, the squirrel with a little white patch on his chest slugged the other squirrel across the face. Well, this caused the other squirrel to become so enraged that he bit the other squirrel on the tail.

With his tail firmly in the mouth of the other squirrel, white patch started to run off dragging the other squirrel along the way. It was a funny sight seeing the two appearing to play follow the leader, as they tumbled and rolled along the grass. Just as it looked like they would go on forever, white patch whipped around and grabbed the other squirrel's tail by his teeth.

Well, a funnier sight you will never see as they began to roll like a small furry wheel along the grass, chattering loudly as they rolled, neither on willing to let go of the other's tail. All this excitement caused most of the other squirrels to stop gathering nuts, and instead sit on their haunches watching the spectacle unfold before their eyes.

Like all good shows that at some time must come to an end, the two squirrels rolled into a tree and abruptly released each other's tail. They sat there for a moment looking at each other in the eye, as if to say that they had enough, and then scampered off into the woods. If you listened closely, you might have heard a slight applause from the furry spectators around the leafy stage.

The Night Stalker

In the dark shadows of the trees, the huge owl turns its face from me. Not in shyness but in anger that I have intruded into his sanctuary, where he alone rules the night.

His golden round eyes pierce the darkness of the night into my very soul, as if to say that I must have better things to do than disrupt his hunt.

Disregarding his intimidating stare, I focused my camera on his magnificent body, hoping to capture one of nature's finest in his natural habitat. Reacting to the flash, his eyes glowed like Dante's inferno, expelling rage at my intrusion into his dark domain.

His action was swift and loud, he puffed up his large body, his feathers almost standing straight out as he began to hoot and hoot. He continued to hoot as his head turned side to side, keeping his burning eyes focused on me as though I was his intended prey.

Suddenly in disgust, or as it seemed, the owl lifted itself into the air as it turned its hungry, hooked beak upon me. The long sheath of its wings became the perfect, flying machine as it glided through the air like a knife.

If by some miracle we speak the same language, what is it that I could say that would convince him that I was sorry for the disruption of his night.

So, I cannot undue upon what happened that night, not self-admonition, or blame, and not recrimination. But know as the moon rises and sets, the owl in all its splendor will continue to hunt in the dark shadows of the night.

At the end of the night, he will soar away into the crooked branches of the trees, preening his feathered coat under the silver moon on its way to another morning, after all, he is the stalker of the night.

The Soaring Geese

A cross the land something comes soaring, a sleek and silent object, covered with tan feathers. It moves on invisible muscles as though time did not exist, as though

It was happiest when its wings were extended and flying through the air.

And now it turns its dark eyes, adjusting the feathers of its wings, trailing a well designed web feet. It will soon arrive, leading the way as the rest of the flock trails behind beating their wings to stay in formation.

The geese land like jet planes on an aircraft carrier, gear down, flaps down, tails dragging like hooks on a plane hoping to catch the landing wire. The geese gather to map out their next flight plan, loudly expressing their vocal concerns to all who would listen.

As I listen to their inner circle squawking, I interpret their honks to mean that you do not have to be great to fly. You just have to flap your wings quickly, and let the soft feathered body do what it loves to do.

Meanwhile the sun and the clouds are moving across the land, the cloud's shadows mirroring the flight of the geese as they soar high in the sky, on their way to some distant land.

So, whoever we are, no matter where we are, the world offers itself to our imagination, calls us to us like the geese, harsh and exciting, let our souls soar.

Six Little Guinea Pigs

L isten up now, let me have your undivided attention as I tell you a tale of the guinea pigs. You might ask what is a guinea pig? Well; they are a small stout bodied short eared nearly tailless domesticated rodent, often kept as pets.

But these were not ordinary guinea pigs, no sir, they could talk, squeal, laugh, cry, eat, man could they eat, and other unmentionable functions. They were proud pets of one Ms. Sarah, who adopted all six of them and treated them as part of the family. Well, enough of the introductions, perhaps we should get on with why these little pigs are different from the rest of the guinea pigs of the world.

When Ms. Sarah first brought them home, she set out to name them, which was not an easy task. 'Oh' by the way, did I mention that there was six of them, wow! Anyway, she set out to observe them, to study their personalities before she named them.

Ms. Sarah knew that one of them was the momma pig, and observed that she was overly sweet, so she named her Momma, brilliant, right! Number two pig was cute, and laid back, so she named her Precious, 'Oh' and number three pig was highly active and the color of chocolate, so she named her Fudgy, appropriate, right! Number four pig was very bossy, always giving orders to the other pigs, so she named her Lucy, why I do not know! Number five pig was very vocal and chewed on everything, did I mention she is blonde, maybe that is why she named her Eliana. Number six pig, glad this is the last one, whew! She was the youngest one, 'Ah', so she named her summer.

Well, now that we covered that part of the story, let us get on to why these little guinea pigs are so interesting.

For months and months Ms. Sarah has been caring for her little family, feeding them, talking to them, even taking them outside for air and exercise. Well, one day the little pigs all got together and decided that they should do something special for Ms. Sarah, seeing as how she has been so nice and loving to them since they became part of the family.

After many days of discussions, maybe I should say squeaking, they decided that they should buy her a gift. No ordinary gift would do for these little pigs, no sir, they wanted something special for her. So, it was decided, or should I say Mama

Pig decided that they should take the pig mobile and go to the local shopping mall.

When they arrived at the shopping mall, they could find no parking, so Lucy said, since we have no tails, let us park in the handicap space, so they did. They then proceeded into the shopping mall to look for some interesting stores, hoping that they could get some good ideas for a gift.

After hours of walking around the shopping mall, and with little legs, that is a fete, pardon the pun, they spied a nice dress shop. Eliana said, vocally, I bet Ms. Sarah would love something from here, and the other five little pigs agreed. Now the hard part was deciding what to get her that she would really like, and Precious said she thought Ms. Sarah would like something sexy, all the others agreed except Mama, who you can guess was somewhat modest. Each one of the little pigs suggested something different, but nothing came up that they all could agree on. Finally, the sales lady suggested that they purchase a gift certificate, that way Ms. Sarah could pick out something that she would really like. So that is what they did, they purchased the gift certificate, got back into their pig mobile, and headed home.

When they got back to their house, there was Ms. Sarah all worried as to where they had gone. She said, I was worried that someone had kidnapped you all or worse, and I was ready to call the police. Mama pig spoke up and explained where and why they had gone to the shopping mall, and apologized for not letting her know, but that they wanted to surprise her.

Once everyone had calmed down, all the little pigs gathered together; Mama, Precious, Fudgy, Lucy, Eliana, and Summer, and said to Ms. Sarah, we have a surprise for you. Ms. Sarah was shocked and excited, and said, you did not have to get me anything. They all said at once, yes, we did, because you have been so sweet and kind to us, we just wanted to thank you for all you have done for us.

With all the "you didn't and yes we did" out of the way, they presented Ms. Sarah with the gift certificate. Ms. Sarah was overwhelmed with joy and gratitude and thanked them all.

So ends our little tale, 'pardon the pun' of the six little guinea pigs, they went back to their cage, tired and happy.

The Visitor

She was there when I arrived home, sitting by the garage door, as though she was waiting for me. It was a dark, damp fall night with a chill hanging in the air as she huddled there with her nose in her paws for warmth. She did not move when I raised the garage door but proceeded to look at me with an expression of familiarity, as though she was expecting me.

I picked her up and placed her over at the side of the door, so that I could drive the car into the garage without running over her. As I got out of the car, she came over to me and began rubbing my leg as though we were old friends. She looked up at me, her eyes were bright as stars under her long lashes. Her little face was a picture of beauty, sort of resembling a small panda bear with a long tail.

I saw shear happiness when I spoke to her, here I felt a soft unforced love from this little ball of gray, white hair. As I opened the door, she scooted in between my legs, and promptly headed for the living room. There on the sofa, she regally sat like a little princess awaiting her court. Between the purrs and quiet meows, I believed she was requesting a snack or beverage, should I be so kind.

After satisfying her desires, she proceeded to explore the house checking out every nook and corner for who knows what. She walked determinately, putting one little paw in front of the other, her tail held high with a hook at the tip as she inspected the premises. Occasionally she would look back at me with her nose held high, as if to say, not bad digs but perhaps a little dusty.

Completing her inspection, which I think passed, she jumped up onto my lap and proceeded to lick my face and ear. I supposed that it was an award for passing the inspection, or perhaps a sign of gratitude for the earlier snack.

Acknowledging that she was probably someone else's pet, I picked her up and gently put her outside to return to her home. The night was silent, and the dark had grown darker as she looked up at the clearing sky. The moon, in its shining silver house, rises, and whatever possessed her to visit will remain a mystery as she stalked into the night.

The Blue- Footed Booby Bird

The Blue-Footed Booby Bird is a comical-looking tropical seabird with bright webbed feet and bluish facial skin. The head of the bird is a pale cinnamon brown with white streaks. On the back of his neck, there is a white patch where the neck connects with the head. The lower breast, central tail feathers and under parts are white. Its blue tapered bill has serrated edges that enables the bird to tightly grasp fish.

The Blue-Footed Booby bird is a little under 3 feet long, and its wingspan is around 5 feet. The bird is native to the Galapagos Islands, where it lives off the fish it catches by plunging headfirst into the ocean.

The name "Booby" comes from the Spanish term "Bubi", which means stupid fellow. This is because the Blue-Footed Boobie is clumsy on land, but exceptionally good when in the air or sea.

The Blue-Footed Booby is best known for its mating dance. The male raises one blue foot in the air, then the other, as he struts in front of the female. His movements make him appear to be dancing as he stamps his blue feet up and down on the ground.

One day a tourist was visiting the Galapagos Islands when she spotted one of the Blue footed Boobies dancing among a group of fellow Boobies, and he was putting on quite a show for them. She watched in amazement as he placed one foot after another in many directions, all the while twisting and turning, jumping up and down flapping his wings. The crowd of fellow Boobies were cheering, or should I say squawking their approval of his performance.

The tourist was so impressed with his dancing, that she videoed his performance for future show and tell her friends. When she returned home and showed the video to her friends, they all were so impressed with the Blue Footed Booby's performance that they said maybe he should be on the show, Dancing with the Stars.

He never had the opportunity to compete on the show, but we do know that he was a star with all of the other Boobies on the Island. He continues to do his dancing with his new mate, and as of today is teaching his little ones how to do the Blue Footed Booby dance step.

About the Author

A resident of Bucks County, Pennsylvania, Patrick spends most of his time between work in the aerospace industry and leisure time spent skiing, golf, Tennis, and flying.

Adventure sparks his interest; whether traveling the country on business or pleasure, he always finds time to see the beauty that nature has provided.